Wolf Child

Written by Susan Gates

Illustrated by Liz Pichon

PUFFIN

To Laura, Alex and Christopher   S.G.
To my wolf boy, Zak   L.P.

PUFFIN BOOKS
Published by the Penguin Group
Penguin Books Ltd, 80 Strand, London WC2R 0RL, England
Penguin Group (USA), Inc., 375 Hudson Street, New York, New York 10014, USA
Penguin Books Australia Ltd, 250 Camberwell Road, Camberwell, Victoria 3124, Australia
Penguin Books Canada Ltd, 10 Alcorn Avenue, Toronto, Ontario, Canada M4V 3B2
Penguin Books India (P) Ltd, 11 Community Centre, Panchsheel Park, New Delhi – 110 017, India
Penguin Group (NZ), cnr Airborne and Rosedale Roads, Albany, Auckland 1310, New Zealand
Penguin Books (South Africa) (Pty) Ltd, 24 Sturdee Avenue, Rosebank 2196, South Africa
Penguin Books Ltd, Registered Offices: 80 Strand, London WC2R 0RL, England

www.penguin.com

First published 2004

1 3 5 7 9 10 8 6 4 2

Text copyright © Susan Gates, 2004
Illustrations copyright © Liz Pichon, 2004
The moral right of the author and illustrator has been asserted

Set in Kosmik-Plain Three
Manufactured in China
British Library Cataloguing in Publication Data
A CIP catalogue record for this book is available from the British Library

ISBN 0–670–91292–1 (Hardback)
ISBN 0–140–56896–4 (Paperback)

Small Wolf liked being a wolf.

He liked doing all the things wolves do.
He stayed up late to howl at the moon.
He wolfed down his food.

He scratched himself
whenever he felt like it.

He slept in a messy cave full of bones.

He sniffed at smelly things.

He piddled
against trees.

Small Wolf thought
being a wolf was great.

UGH!

Then one dark night, something very weird happened.
He saw a shooting star with a fiery tail.
It seemed to fall to earth beside him.

It lit him up with a strange blue glow.
Small Wolf said to himself, "I feel a bit funny!"

Suddenly, he started to change. His hairy paws became smooth hands...

his ten long claws became ten pink fingernails...

his ears and tail started shrinking...

then he stood
up on two legs!

He looked at himself in a forest pond.
"Oh no!" he said. "I've changed into a boy!"

Small Wolf had no idea what boys did. He crept up to a house to see if he could find out.

There was a boy inside and his mum and dad were talking to him. Small Wolf listened very carefully.

"Children are supposed to wash behind their ears and tidy their rooms!" the boy's mum was saying in a strict voice. "And change their socks!"

"Socks!" thought Small Wolf. "I'd better get some of those."

"Children must never, ever wolf down their food," the boy's dad was saying.
"Yes, and they're not supposed to fidget," added the boy's mum.

Boys should sit still and be quiet!

Boys should have lovely manners!

"So that's what boys do,"
thought Small Wolf. "Well, now I'm a boy,
that's what I must do too."
He grabbed some socks from the washing
line – and other clothes to keep warm – and
hurried off home.

He went back home to his wolf mum and dad who gave him a good sniff. They looked amazed, "Are you really our son?"

"Yes, it's really me," said Small Wolf. "This star thing came from outer space. It changed me into a boy. But don't worry, I know exactly what to do."

And he began
tidying up their
messy cave.

"But we like our cave messy," said Mrs Wolf.
"I'm a boy now," Small Wolf told her. "And children
are *never* messy."

He's too clean...

Small Wolf started doing all the other things that he'd heard boys are supposed to do. He stopped wolfing down his food and took tiny nibbles. He even told his dad off.
"Must you wolf food down like that?
You should never gobble!"

DISGUSTING!

And he told his mum off.
"Mum," he said sternly.
"Do stop sniffing at pongy things and scratching yourself. Where are your manners?"

He washed behind his ears twice a day.

"Dad," he scolded, "did you remember to wash behind your ears? Boys never forget!"

And he never, ever fidgeted. "Mum!" he nagged. "I just saw your tail twitch. You should always sit still!"

He wouldn't even join in when his mum and dad
howled at the moon.

"Parents!" he ordered them. "Do stop that frightful row!
You shouldn't be so noisy!"

This was the last straw. His parents couldn't stand it a second longer. They went to see the Wise Old Wolf.

"We've got this big problem," they said. "Our son has changed into a boy. It's a nightmare! He tells us off all day long!"

"Is that what boys are really like?" Mrs Wolf asked the Wise Old Wolf. "How do their parents put up with it?"

Aren't you wise already?

WISE WOLF IN

"He even wants a toilet in our cave," added Mr Wolf.
"I've begged him and begged him – but he refuses
to piddle up trees any more."
"We want our wild-wolf son back!"
they both complained.

ENGAGED

My
Wolf

"Hmmm," said the Wise Old Wolf. "This is a tricky problem."
He thought for a long time. At last he said, "It's a long shot.
But I've got this magic bone somewhere . . ."

He found the magic bone
and blew the cobwebs off it.
"I haven't used it for a long, long time."
"Magic bone?" said Mr Wolf, frowning.
"Are you kidding me? Will it really work?"

"I've seen it change wolves back into people. But I haven't got a clue if it changes boys back into wolves," admitted the Wise Old Wolf.

"I'll try anything!" cried Mrs Wolf, snatching the bone. "We're desperate!"

They rushed back to their cave.

"Here, son," said Mr Wolf. "Would you like a little snack?"
Naturally, Small Wolf wouldn't gnaw the bone. He just
nibbled it round the edges, very politely, like boys are
supposed to do.

For a few seconds, nothing changed.
"That magic bone's useless," growled Mr Wolf.
"I knew it wouldn't work."
"Oh, no, he's going to stay human," said Mrs Wolf.
"We'd better go and wash behind our ears!"

But then something started to happen. Small Wolf's smooth hands grew hairy again...

his ten pink fingernails became ten long claws...

his hairy ears came back...

and his lovely,
long, hairy tail
reappeared!

He dropped on to all fours
and went trotting out of the cave.

I'm a WOLF again!

"Where are you going?" Mrs Wolf shouted after him. "I'm going to sniff at pongy things and scratch myself!" said Small Wolf.

HOORAY!

Mr Wolf hardly dared hope. Had his wolf son really come back?
Then Small Wolf rushed up to the nearest tree.
"Oh, joy!" cried Mr Wolf. "He's piddling up trees again!"

Small Wolf loped off to howl at the moon.
"Welcome back, son!" said Mrs Wolf.